The Mystery of Irma Vep

A Penny Dreadful

by Charles Ludlam

A SAMUEL FRENCH ACTING EDITION

SAMUEL FRENCH

FOUNDED 1830

New York Hollywood London Toronto

SAMUELFRENCH.COM

in

THE MYSTERY OF IRMA VEP

A Penny Dreadful

Written and Directed by
CHARLES LUDLAM

starring

CHARLES LUDLAM and **EVERETT QUINTON**

Settings by	*Costumes by*	*Lighting by*
CHARLES LUDLAM	**EVERETT QUINTON**	**LAWRENCE EICHLER**

Original Music Composed by
PETER GOLUB

CAST
(in order of appearance)

Jane Twisden	EVERETT QUINTON
Nicodemus Underwood	CHARLES LUDLAM
Lady Enid Hillcrest	CHARLES LUDLAM
Lord Edgar Hillcrest	EVERETT QUINTON
An Intruder	EVERETT QUINTON
Alcazar	CHARLES LUDLAM
Irma Vep	? ? ?

ACT I
Mandacrest, on the moors

ACT II
Various places in Egypt

ACT III
Mandacrest

THERE WILL BE A FIFTEEN-MINUTE INTERMISSION AFTER ACT I.

4

Cast of Characters

Lady Enid Hillcrest
Lord Edgar Hillcrest
Nicodemus Underwood
Jane Twisden
An intruder
Irma Vep

The action of the play takes place in the library drawing room of "Mandacrest," the Hillcrest estate near Hampstead Heath, between the wars; and various places in Egypt.

Note: THE MYSTERY OF IRMA VEP is a full-length quick-change act. All roles are portrayed by two performers.

The Mystery of Irma Vep

ACT I

SCENE 1

(*The study is a large room with French doors at the back that open out on a garden. There is a desk and chair. A fireplace with a mantel over which is a portrait of Lady Irma in her bloom. Two deep armchairs flank the fireplace. There are signs that the Hillcrests have travelled: African masks, an Egyptian mummy case, and a painted Japanese screen. There is a bookcase with morocco bound volumes and doors left and right. At rise Nicodemus enters from the garden, through the French doors, carrying a basket. His left leg is deformed and the sole of his shoe is built up with wood. Jane is arranging flowers in a bowl.*)

JANE. Watch what you're doing! You're soaking wet! Don't track mud in here!

NICODEMUS. It's God's good rain, my girl.

JANE. It's the devil's rain. That's what it is!

(*Lightning flashes, then thunder is heard.*)

NICODEMUS. Would you rather the drought went on and on? It's thankful you should be. And that mightily.

JANE. And don't clump so with that wooden leg. You'll wake Lady Enid.

NICODEMUS. And wasn't it to save Lord Edgar from the wolf that me leg got mangled so? I should think she'd be glad to hear me clump after what I did for him.

JANE. That was a long time ago. Lady Enid doesn't know anything about it.

NICODEMUS. She'll find out soon enough.

JANE. Now, now, Nicodemus, I won't have you frightening Lord Edgar's new bride with your wolf tales.

NICODEMUS. And the sooner she does find out the better, I say!

JANE. Hush. Your tongue will dig your grave, Nicodemus. There are some things better left unsaid.

NICODEMUS. Pah! It's a free country, ain't it?

JANE. Shhh!

NICODEMUS. Well, ain't it?

JANE. If Lord Edgar hears you you'll see how free it is. You'll find yourself without a situation.

NICODEMUS. That's a little bit too free for me. I'll bite me tongue.

JANE. We must stand by Lord Edgar. I'm afraid he'll be needing us now more than ever.

NICODEMUS. Why now more than ever? I'd say the worst was over. He's finally accepted the fact that Miss Irma's in her grave.

JANE. Don't talk like that. I can't bear the thought of her in a grave. She was always so afraid of the dark.

NICODEMUS. He's accepted it and you must too. Life has begun again for him. He mourned a more than respectable length of time and now he's brought home a new Lady Hillcrest.

JANE. That's just it. That's just the very thing! I don't think Lady Enid will ever make a fit mistress for Mandacrest.

NICODEMUS. And why not?

JANE. She's so, so—common. She'll never live up to the high standard set by Lady Irma.

NICODEMUS. That my girl is not for you or me to decide.

JANE. I can't stand the thought of taking orders from that vulgarian.

NICODEMUS. Come come, I won't have you talking that way about Lady Enid.

JANE. Lady Irma had a commanding presence and her manners were impeccable.

NICODEMUS. It takes more to please a man than fancy manners.

JANE. I would think a man—a *real* man would find nothing more pleasing than fine breeding and savoir fair.

NICODEMUS. If that French means what I think it does you'd better wash your mouth out with soap. Here's eggs and milk. The turtle was laying rather well today.

JANE. And where's the cream?

NICODEMUS. I skimmed it.

JANE. Again? Ah, you're incorrigible.

NICODEMUS. In what?

JANE. Now what will I tell Lord Edgar when he wants cream for his tea, huh?

NICODEMUS. Tell him what you like.

(*Lightning and a clap of thunder.*)

JANE. (*Shrieks*) Ahhh!

NICODEMUS. There there. Don't be skeered. Nicodemus is here to protect you. (*Tries to put his arm around her.*)

JANE. (*Eluding his embrace*) Keep your hands to yourself. You smell like a stable.

NICODEMUS. If you slept in a stable you'd smell like one too.

JANE. Keep your distance.

NICODEMUS. Someday, Janey my girl, you're going to smile on me.

JANE. Yeah, when hell freezes over and little devils go ice skating.

NICODEMUS. If I was cleaned up and had a new white

collar and smelled of bay rum and Florida Water you'd think different.

JANE. Don't you get any ideas about me. You are beneath me and beneath me you're going to stay.

NICODEMUS. Someday you might want to get beneath me.

JANE. UGH! How dare you speak to me in such a manner. I've had education.

NICODEMUS. What education have you ever had?

JANE. I've read Bunyan's *Pilgrim's Progress* from cover to cover, the *Holy Bible*, the almanac and several back issues of Godey's Ladies' Book.

NICODEMUS. Well I've read the Swineherd's Manual from kiver to kiver.

JANE. (*Contemptuously*) Hurmph!

NICODEMUS. You got no reason to look down your nose at me, Miss. We're cut from the same bolt o' goods.

JANE. Don't go giving yourself airs. Go on back to your pigsty before I say something I'll be sorry for.

NICODEMUS. I'm not leaving until you give me a kiss.

JANE. I'll see you hanged first.

NICODEMUS. (*Chasing her around the room*) Give me a little kiss and then I'll show you how I'm hung.

JANE. Get away from me you beast with your double entendres.

NICODEMUS. Double what?

(*Thunder, footsteps above.*)

JANE. Now you've done it. You've waked Lady Enid. Go quick before she sees you in the house.

NICODEMUS. What's she getting up now for? It's just about evening.

JANE. That's her way. She sleeps all day and she's up all night.

NICODEMUS. It's them city ways of hers. Lord Edgar told me she'd been on the stage.

JANE. (*Shocked*) The stage! Ugh! How disgusting!

NICODEMUS. To think, a real live actress here at Mandacrest!

JANE. Yes, it's utterly degrading. But she is the mistress of the house now and we must adjust to her ways.

NICODEMUS. That's not what I meant. I think Lord Edgar has really done well for himself.

JANE. You men are all alike. You're so easily taken in. (*Footsteps*) I hear her footsteps. Go!

NICODEMUS. But I want to get a look at her.

JANE. She's just an ordinary woman and she doesn't need you gawking at her. Go on back to your pigsty.

NICODEMUS. I found better company there than ever I found at Mandacrest. (*Exits*)

LADY ENID'S VOICE. (*Off*) Jane, were you talking to someone?

JANE. Just Nicodemus. He came to bring the eggs.

LADY ENID. (*Off*) Is he gone?

JANE. Yes, Lady Enid.

LADY ENID. Has the sun set?

JANE. It's pouring down rain, your Ladyship. There's very little out there that could be called sun.

LADY ENID. Draw the draperies and light a fire. I'm coming down.

JANE. Ah Lord, my work is never done. (*Draws the draperies across the French doors, cutting off the view of the garden. She takes a quick look at herself in the mirror; fans herself with her handkerchief; straightens her hair and collar; then lights the fire.*)

LADY ENID. (*Entering*) Ah, you've made the room warm and cheery. Thank you, Jane.

JANE. Can I fix you a nice cup of tea?

LADY ENID. If it's no trouble.

JANE. (*Sternly*) That's what I'm here for.

LADY ENID. Is Lord Edgar about?

JANE. He was up and out at the crack of dawn.

LADY ENID. Out? Out where?

JANE. He goes riding in the morning. It's a custom with him. (*Tea kettle whistles off.*) Ah, there's the kettle calling. (*Exits*)

LADY ENID. (*Looks about the room and examines the paintings and books. She looks out the French doors into the garden and out to the moors beyond. Then the portrait over the mantel catches her attention. She stands before it and stares at it a long time.*)

JANE. (*Returning with the tea things*) How do you take it?

LADY ENID. I beg your pardon?

JANE. Your tea, Miss.

LADY ENID. Plain.

JANE. (*Incredulous*) No cream or sugar?

LADY ENID. No, quite plain.

JANE. That's queer.

LADY ENID. Queer?

JANE. Tea ain't much without cream and sugar.

LADY ENID. I'm on an eternal diet. The stage you know.

JANE. But that's all behind you now.

LADY ENID. (*With a sigh*) Yes, I suppose it is. But the habit's ingrained. I shall probably refuse bread and potatoes 'til I die. (*Indicating the portrait.*) Who is that woman?

JANE. Why, that's Lady Hillcrest . . . I mean, that's the last Lady Hillcrest.

LADY ENID. She was very beautiful, wasn't she?

JANE. There will never be another woman who's her equal—oh, I beg your pardon, Miss.

LADY ENID. That's alright, Jane. You were very fond

of her, weren't you?

JANE. (*Bringing her a cup of tea*) She was like a part of meself, Miss.

LADY ENID. I see. (*Sits and sips tea. Sharp reaction to the tea.*) You do make strong tea, don't you?

JANE. (*Indignant*) When I makes tea I makes tea. And when I makes water I makes water.

LADY ENID. God send you don't make them in one pot.

JANE. (*Beat. Then realizing that a joke was made at her expense*) Hurmph!

LADY ENID. You don't like me, do you, Jane?

JANE. I don't hate you.

LADY ENID. I should hope not! That would be a terrible thing, wouldn't it? If you hated me and we had to live here together.

JANE. Yes, I suppose it would. I said I don't hate you.

LADY ENID. You don't hate me. But you don't like me.

JANE. I'm not used to you. You'll take getting used to.

LADY ENID. (*Shivers*) I felt a chill. A cat walked over my grave.

JANE. Isn't there a draft there, where you're sitting, Lady Enid?

LADY ENID. Yes, there is a little. Perhaps you'd better close the French doors.

JANE. Did Nicodemus leave them open again? If I've told him once I've told him a thousand times . . . Why isn't that the master coming over there?

LADY ENID. (*Quickly*) Where? (*Gets up.*) Yes, it's he. (*Hiding behind the curtain.*) Stand back! Don't let him see us.

JANE. What's that he's carrying? Armsful of heather and he's dragging something behind.

LADY ENID. Dragging something?

JANE. It looks like a big animal. Why, I believe he's killed the wolf.

LADY ENID. (*Nervously*) Wolf?

JANE. The wolf that's been killing our lambs. Well we'll all sleep better too without that devil howling all night.

LADY ENID. He killed a wolf?

JANE. Yes, and he's brought the carcass back with him.

LADY ENID. Is it dead? Is it really dead?

JANE. It's dead and it won't get any deader.

LADY ENID. Which way is he coming?

JANE. He's taking the path by the pyracanthas.

LADY ENID. He's done that before. But will he take the footbridge?

JANE. That's just what I was asking meself. He's getting closer — no he's turned off — he's going the long way 'round and through the ivy arches.

LADY ENID. Then he's still not over it.

JANE. Ah, you can't blame him for not taking the footbridge after what happened there.

LADY ENID. They cling to their dead a long time at Mandacrest.

JANE. Nay, I think it's the dead that cling to us. It's as if they just don't want to let go. Like they can't bear to leave us behind. (*Comes back to herself abruptly.*) The master will be wanting his dinner. (*Turning at the door.*) How do you like your meat, Miss?

LADY ENID. Well done.

JANE. No red meat?

LADY ENID. Not for me.

JANE. See, there's another difference. Miss Irma liked it bloody. (*Exits*)

LADY ENID. (*Turns sharply and looks at the portrait*)

Don't look at me like that. I didn't take him away from you, you know. Someone was apt to take your place sooner or later. It happened to be me. I know how you must feel seeing us so happy under your very nose. But there's nothing to be done about it, old girl. Life must go on.

(*Enter Lord Edgar.*)

LORD EDGAR. (*With armsful of heather, dragging wolf carcass as described*) Rough weather.

LADY ENID. (*Rushing to Edgar and planting a kiss on his lips*) Edgar, darling, you're back.

LORD EDGAR. Please, Enid, not in front of . . .

LADY ENID. In front of who? There's no one looking. (*Pauses*) Unless you mean her. (*Points to the painting.*)

LORD EDGAR. It does seem a bit odd. I mean kissing right in front of her.

LADY ENID. She looks vaguely sinister.

LORD EDGAR. Please, Enid. She's dead.

LADY ENID. Perhaps that's the reason.

LORD EDGAR. Let's don't talk about her.

LADY ENID. Yes, let's don't.

LORD EDGAR. Are you quite comfortable?

LADY ENID. Yes, quite. Jane doesn't like me but I think I'll win her over.

LORD EDGAR. I hope you'll like it here.

LADY ENID. I'm sure I will. Oh, Edgar, Edgar.

LORD EDGAR. Oh, Enid, Enid.

LADY ENID. Oh Wedgar, Wedgar, Wedgar.

LORD EDGAR. Oh Wenid, Wenid, Wenid.

LADY ENID. (With a qualm) Edgar.

LORD EDGAR. (*Slightly reprimanding*) Enid.

LADY ENID. (*Reassured*) Edgar.

LORD EDGAR. (*Condescendingly*) Enid.

LADY ENID. (*Snuggling his chest, with a sigh*) Edgar Edgar Edgar.

LORD EDGAR. (*Comforting and comfortable*) Enid Enid Enid.

LADY ENID. (*Passionately*) Edgar!

LORD EDGAR. (*Aroused*) Enid!

LADY ENID. (*More passionately*) Edgar!

LORD EDGAR. (*More passionately*) Enid!

LADY ENID. (*Rapturously*) Edgar!

LORD EDGAR. (*Likewise*) Enid!

LADY ENID. (*Climactically*) Edgar!!

LORD EDGAR. (*Orgasmically*) Enid!!

LADY ENID. (*Cooing*) Edgar.

LORD EDGAR. (*Drowsily*) Enid.

LADY ENID. Edgar?

LORD EDGAR. Enid.

LADY ENID. Take the painting down.

LORD EDGAR. I couldn't do that.

LADY ENID. Why not?

LORD EDGAR. I just couldn't.

LADY ENID. She's been dead three years.

LORD EDGAR. Yes, I know, but . . .

LADY ENID. Let's make a fresh start. Forget about the past.

LORD EDGAR. I want to, Enid, believe me, I do.

LADY ENID. We'll never feel comfortable with her watching every move we make.

LORD EDGAR. No, I suppose not.

LADY ENID. Then, why not put her things away in a chest somewhere or make a little shrine where you can visit her once in a while? But not our home.

LORD EDGAR. You're right of course. I know you are. It's just that . . .

LADY ENID. What?

LORD EDGAR. She made me promise that I would always keep a flame burning before her picture.

LADY ENID. What nonsense.

LORD EDGAR. I tell you she made me promise.

LADY ENID. Blow it out.

LORD EDGAR. I couldn't break my word.

LADY ENID. I thought you belonged to me now. That we belonged to each other.

LORD EDGAR. We do, but that was before we met.

LADY ENID. Which means more to you? Your love for me or your promise to her?

LORD EDGAR. Enid, please. Don't put it that way.

LADY ENID. Which is it, Edgar? Which will it be?

LORD EDGAR. Please don't make me choose.

LADY ENID. Do you love me?

LORD EDGAR. How can you doubt it?

LADY ENID. Then the choice is already made. Blow it out!

LORD EDGAR. Dare I? (*Blows out the candle.*)

LADY ENID. You see, nothing happened.

LORD EDGAR. Weird that we thought it would.

(*They laugh.*)

LADY ENID. And now, darling, as to this matter of dragging dead animals into the drawing room — it's really got to stop.

LORD EDGAR. I say, you're really out to reform me, aren't you?

LADY ENID. Just a little.

LORD EDGAR. I'll have Nicodemus tend to it. Why don't you change for dinner?

LADY ENID. Good. I'm famished.

LORD EDGAR. Don't be long.

LADY ENID. I won't, I promise. (*Exits*)

LORD EDGAR. (*Goes to the painting*) Forgive me, Irma, please. Please forgive me!

(*Enter Nicodemus.*)

NICODEMUS. Where is the new lady?

LORD EDGAR. Changing. You know how slow women are.

NICODEMUS. So you've finally killed the beast, eh, Lord Edgar.

LORD EDGAR. Yes, I've killed it. It will rage no more.

NICODEMUS. But what about the beast within? Is that through with raging?

LORD EDGAR. It's resting peacefully at the moment. That's about the most we can expect, don't you think?

NICODEMUS. You're a man of will, you are, Edgar Hillcrest.

LORD EDGAR. Nicodemus, take the guts out and burn it.

NICODEMUS. Don't you want to save the skin?

LORD EDGAR. No, burn every hide and hair of it.

NICODEMUS. And the ashes? What should I do with them?

LORD EDGAR. Scatter them on the heath.

NICODEMUS. And let the wind take up its howling?

LORD EDGAR. Then throw them in the mill run.

NICODEMUS. After her?

LORD EDGAR. Yes, after her. And Nicodemus . . .

NICODEMUS. Yes, Lord Edgar?

LORD EDGAR. Take down the painting.

NICODEMUS. And what do you want me to do with it?

LORD EDGAR. Burn it with the wolf. (*Exits*)

(*Underwood goes toward the mantel and tries to take down the painting. Enter Jane.*)

JANE. And what do you think you're doing?

NICODEMUS. The master wants the painting down.

JANE. You can't do that. You can't take Lady Irma!

NICODEMUS. I can and I will. It's the Master's orders.

JANE. Stop it! Stop it! Don't touch that picture. Ahgh! The sanctuary light's gone out. Oh God, this will never do.

NICODEMUS. Don't blame me. It was out when I came in. Lord Edgar must have extinguished it.

JANE. (*Indicating the carcass*) And what's this here?

NICODEMUS. You've got eyes in your head to see with. It's the wolf. He's killed the wolf.

JANE. Glory be! Is it possible?

NICODEMUS. It's cause for rejoicing.

JANE. (*Approaching the carcass warily*) It's no rejoicing there'll be this night, Nicodemus Underwood. He's killed the wrong wolf.

(*Blackout.*)

SCENE 2

The scene is as before. It is late evening. The household is asleep. Jane is stoking the last embers of the fire. Lady Enid enters silently in her dressing gown. She stands over Jane, whose back is to her, and watches. Jane suddenly becomes aware of her presence and, frightened, gasps. This in turn frightens Lady Enid, who gasps also.

LADY ENID. I didn't mean to frighten you.

JANE. I didn't mean to frighten you either. You shouldn't creep up on a person like that.

LADY ENID. I'm sorry, Jane. You have lived here a considerable time. Did you not say sixteen years?

JANE. Eighteen, Miss; I came when the mistress was married, to wait on her; after she died, the master retained me as his housekeeper. Though I knew him from childhood. I was raised at the Frambly Parsonage.

LADY ENID. Indeed.

(*Long silence between them.*)

JANE. Ah, times have greatly changed since then!

LADY ENID. Yes, you've seen a good many alterations, I suppose?

JANE. I have; and troubles too.

LADY ENID. The Hillcrests are a very old family, aren't they?

JANE. Oh, Lord, yes. Why the Hillcrests go back to . . . back to . . . well, I don't know exactly who. But they've been descending for centuries.

LADY ENID. Lord Edgar told me he was an only child.

JANE. Yes, a strange flower upon the old solid wood of the family tree.

LADY ENID. Was he always so fond of hunting, even as a child?

JANE. Nay, he only took that up after the mistress passed away. Oh, but that's a long story. I won't be after boring you with it.

LADY ENID. Oh, do go on, Jane. Everything about Lord Edgar fascinates me.

JANE. Where is himself?

LADY ENID. Sleeping soundly. Jane, it will be an act of

charity to tell me something of the family history. I know I shall not be able to rest if I go to bed, so be good enough to sit and chat for an hour.

JANE. Oh, certainly, Miss! I'll just fetch a little sewing and then I'll sit as long as you please. Listen to that wind! It's an ungodly night. Can I get you a hot toddy to drive out the cold?

LADY ENID. If you're having one.

JANE. Sure I loves me toddy and me toddy loves me.

(*She crosses to the table, gets her sewing, and pours out two toddies from a pan she has nestled among the embers. She gives one drink to Lady Enid and settles into the chair opposite her before the fire. Howling sound.*)

LADY ENID. That wind!

JANE. That's not the wind. That's a wolf howling.

LADY ENID. It seems you've been troubled by wolves of late.

JANE. Not wolves. It's one wolf in particular. Victor.

LADY ENID. Victor?

JANE. He was captured as a pup and tamed. But his heart was savage. Miss Irma kept him as a pet.

LADY ENID. Like a dog.

JANE. He was bigger than a dog; so big the boy used to ride about on his back. Though Victor didn't like that much, I can tell you. Though he bore it for the mistress' sake, for it was to her he belonged. His happiest hours were spent stretched out at Miss Irma's feet, his huge purple tongue lolling out of his mouth. He never left her side the whole time she was carrying. Lord Edgar locked him out when it came time for her to deliver. And when he heard her labor pains, he howled.

LADY ENID. Lord Edgar told me that he'd had a son but that he died when he was still a child.

JANE. Ah, there's a tragic story, Miss. But your toddy's gettin' cold. Finish that and I'll fix you another.

LADY ENID. (*Drains her cup and passes it to Jane*) He was taken off with chicken pox, wasn't he?

JANE. Chicken pox? Now who told you that?

LADY ENID. No one told me. I was just supposing.

JANE. If Lord Edgar told you it was chicken pox, then chicken pox it was. We'd better leave it at chicken pox.

LADY ENID. No, really, he didn't tell me anything. The chicken pox was pure conjecture.

JANE. It's understandable that he didn't go into it. It's not an easy subject to talk about. Here's your toddy.

LADY ENID. Thanks.

JANE. And here's one for me.

LADY ENID. I'd like to know the true history, if you don't mind relating it.

JANE. (*The toddy loosening her tongue*) One clear winter day Victor and the boy went out to the heath to play in the new fallen snow. The wolf came back without the boy. We waited. We watched. We called ourselves hoarse. And at dusk we found him in the mill run, dead. His throat had been torn apart.

LADY ENID. Horrible.

JANE. Lord Edgar wanted Victor destroyed. But Lady Irma fought against it. She said it wasn't Vic had done it.

LADY ENID. Perhaps it wasn't.

JANE. His throat was torn. What else could it have been? They fought bitterly over it. He said she loved the wolf more than her own child. But I think it was the double loss she dreaded, for when Victor was gone she'd have nothing, you see. When the Master came to shoot Victor, Lady Irma turned him loose upon the heath and drove him away with stones, crying run, Vic, run, and never come back! I don't think the poor beast understood what happened because he still comes back to this day, looking for Lady Irma.

LADY ENID. Poor Victor. Poor boy. Poor Irma.

JANE. Poor Lord Edgar.

LADY ENID. Yes, poor poor Lord Edgar!

JANE. But here's the strangest part of all.

LADY ENID. Yes?

JANE. The fresh snow is like a map. I traced their tracks meself. Victor's trail turned off. The boy was killed by a wolf that left human tracks in the snow.

LADY ENID. Human? You mean the boy was murdered?

JANE. But that takes us to the subject of werewolves.

LADY ENID. Werewolves?

JANE. Humans who take the form of a wolf at night.

LADY ENID. But that's just superstition.

JANE. Yes, superstition, the realm beyond the explainable where science is powerless. Of course everything pointed to Victor. The boy fell down and skinned his knee. He let the loving beast lick his wound. He tasted blood. The killer was aroused. He turned on the child and sank his fangs into its tender neck. A perfectly logical explanation. But then there were those tracks in the snow. Wouldn't it be convenient for a werewolf to have a real wolf to blame it on?

LADY ENID. Didn't you show them to anyone? The tracks, I mean.

JANE. Ah, they wouldn't listen. They said they were my tracks. That I'd made them meself. I didn't push it, Miss, or they'd have packed me off to Dottyville. It's hard to convince people of the supernatural. Most people have enough trouble believing in the natural.

LADY ENID. Of course you're right. But those footprints.

JANE. I wish I had 'em here as evidence. But where are the snows of yesteryear? And that's the werewolf's greatest alibi — people don't believe in him. Well Miss, I must be gettin' meself to bed. My rheumatism is starting to act up again.

LADY ENID. Leave the light, Jane. I think I'll stay up and read a while.

JANE. Here's a good book for you. It's the master's treatise on ancient Egyptian mythology.

LADY ENID. Thanks!

JANE. Don't stay up too late now. We're having kippers and kidneys for breakfast and I know you wouldn't want to miss that.

LADY ENID. Jane, what was the boy's name?

JANE. Didn't you know? That was Victor too. Goodnight, Lady Enid. (*Exits*)

LADY ENID. (*Sits in chair with her back to the glass doors and reads. The shadow of the stranger can be seen through the sheer organdy curtains illuminated intermittently by flashes of lightning. A boney almost skeletal hand feels for a latch. It drums its fingernails against the windowpane.*) What — what was it? Real or a delusion? Oh God, what was it?

(*Suddenly a single pane of the French door shatters. The boney hand reaches in through the curtains and opens the latch. A gaunt figure enters the room slowly. A ray of light strikes the pallid face. He fixes her with a stare.*)

LADY ENID. Who are you? What do you want?

(*The clock chimes one.
The intruder emits a hissing sound.*)

LADY ENID. What do you want? Oh God, what do you want of me?

(*She tries to run to the door but the intruder catches her by her long hair and, winding it around his boney fingers, drags her back toward the mantel. She takes roses from the vase and presses their thorns into his eyes. The intruder groans and releases her. She runs across the room. He follows her. She stabs him with scissors from Jane's sewing basket. Intruder staggers back and falls through open door down right. Lady Enid crosses to the mantle and tries to get control of herself. She sighs with relief. Intruder reenters and clapping his hand over her mouth drags her to the door, locks it, then crosses up center to the double doors where shriek follows strangled shriek as he seizes her neck in his fang-like teeth and a hideous sucking noise follows. Lady Enid emits a high-pitched scream made at the back of the throat by drawing the breath in. Running footsteps are heard Off.*)

LORD EDGAR. (*Off right*) Did you hear a scream, Jane?
JANE. (*Off right*) I did. Where was it?
LORD EDGAR. (*Off*) God knows. It sounded so near yet far away. I got up and got dressed as soon as I heard it.
JANE. (*Off. No pause*) All is still now.
LORD EDGAR. (*Off*) Yes, but unless I was dreaming there was a scream.
JANE. We couldn't both have dreamed it.
LORD EDGAR. Where's Lady Enid?
JANE. Isn't she with you?

(*Lady Enid emits another high-pitched scream.*)

LORD EDGAR. There it is again. Search the house! Search the house. Where did it come from? Can you tell?

(*Lady Enid screams again as before.*)

LORD EDGAR. Good God! There it is again! (*He tries the door from offstage right. But it will not open.*)
LORD EDGAR. Enid! Enid! Are you in there? Speak for heaven's sake! Speak! Good God we must force the door. (*They beat on the door.*)
LORD EDGAR. Get the crowbar.
JANE. Where is it?
LORD EDGAR. In the cellar. Hurry! Hurry! Run! Run! Enid! Oh Enid!
JANE. Here it is. (*They force the door open and Lord Edgar bursts into the room.*)
NICODEMUS. (*Voice Off, up center*) Lady Enid! Lady Enid! Oh God no! Lady Enid! (*Nicodemus enters carrying the limp body of Lady Enid. Her long hair hangs down covering her face. There are several drops of blood on her nightgown.*) Help oh help oh heaven oh help! (*He carries her body out the door stage right.*) Now where the blue hell am I bringing her, beyond the veil?
LORD EDGAR. (*Following them*) What is it? What's happened? Who's done this thing to you?
NICODEMUS. (*Reentering*) Who or what? I saw something moving in the heath.
LORD EDGAR. Something? What kind of something?
NICODEMUS. Dog's skull. Dog's body. Its glazing eyes staring out of death candle to shake and bend my soul.

(*Suddenly something with a horrible face appears at the window. It lets out a frightening earsplitting sound and then, laughing, bangs against the windowpanes.*)

NICODEMUS. (*Growling in a hoarsened raspy voice*) There! There it is.

(*The thing emits a shrill laugh like the sound of electronic feedback.*)

LORD EDGAR. Lord help us!

NICODEMUS. Be it whatever thing it may — I'll follow it!

LORD EDGAR. No! No! Do not!

NICODEMUS. I must! I will!

LORD EDGAR. Not without a gun! Don't be a fool!

NICODEMUS. Let whoever will come with me — I'll follow this dread form! (*Exits*)

LORD EDGAR. Wait for me you fool! (*Takes a gun from off the wall.*)

NICODEMUS. (*Voice Off*) I see it! I see it! It goes down the wall and through the wisterias.

LORD EDGAR. It's dark down there. There isn't any moon.

(*There are animal sounds; the sounds of a struggle and then a few agonized cries. The doors fly open and a human leg, one that had formerly belonged to Nicodemus, is thrown in.*)

LORD EDGAR. Great Scott! (*He rushes out. And is heard calling Off.*) Which way? Which way?

NICODEMUS. (*Voice Off*) Over here. Help! Oh help me!

(*There is the sound of shots Off.*)

JANE. (*Entering from stage right*) Was them shots I heard?

LADY ENID. (*Sticking her head in through the door stage right*) Jane. Jane.

JANE. Yes Lady Enid.

LADY ENID. Come. I need you. I'm afraid to be alone. (*Withdraws*)

JANE. I'll come and I'll bring the ghost candle to light your agony. It's the curse of the Druids that's what it is. The Druidy Druids. (*Withdraws*)

(*Footsteps and the sound of something dragging.*)

NICODEMUS. (*Entering up center*) I saw it. I touched it. I struggled with it. It was cold and clammy like a corpse. It can't be human.

LORD EDGAR. (*Entering under Nicodemus' arm*) Not human? No, of course not human. You said it was a dog.

NICODEMUS. Then it looked like a wolf, then it looked like a woman! It tore off me leg and started chewing on it.

LORD EDGAR. Great Scott! It can't be.

NICODEMUS. If it hadn't been wood I swear it would have eaten it.

LORD EDGAR. No!

NICODEMUS. Yes! Yes! Ghoul! Chewer of corpses! And all the while it made this disgusting sucking sound. It sucked the very marrow from me bones. I can feel it now. It's very near. Bride bed. Child bed. Bed of death! She comes, pale vampire, through storm her eyes, her batsails bloodying the seas! Mouth to her mouth's kiss! Her eyes on me to strike me down. I felt the green fairy's fang.

(*Howling Off.*)

LORD EDGAR. What was that?

NICODEMUS. Just a wolf.

LORD EDGAR: No! It's Victor! Victor come back to haunt me! (*Starts out*) Give me that pistol there. This time I'll get him! (*Fur at the door*) Look! There it is now! It won't escape this time.

NICODEMUS. (*Clinging to his leg*) No! Master, do not go! There is no help for it!

(*Keening lament is heard on the wind.*)

LORD EDGAR. Let go of my leg. Goblin damned, I'll send your soul to hell! (*Exits*)

NICODEMUS. No! Master! Master! It's Irma, Irma Vep! A ghostwoman with ashes on her breath, alone, crying in the rain.

(*Shots, running footsteps, and howling heard Off.*)

JANE. (*Rushing in*) What's all this yelling? You'll wake the dead.

NICODEMUS. The master's at it again — hunting.

JANE. Is it wolves again?

NICODEMUS. This time he's sure it's Victor.

JANE. Victor?

NICODEMUS. That's what he says!

JANE. Well, don't just stand there gawking! Go after him! Be some help!

NICODEMUS. Oh no. Not me! There's something on that heath that would make your blood run cold.

JANE. Ah, you big sissy. If you don't go to his aid I'll go meself.

NICODEMUS. Oh, very well, woman. Wait until I screw in me leg. [*He goes off, screws it in noisily, returns*]

JANE. It seems that more than your leg got bitten off.

JANE. Let go! Let go! Get out of my way. Lord Edgar needs me.

(*The gun goes off and the bullet hits the painting. The painting bleeds.*)

NICODEMUS. Now see what you've done. You've shot Lady Irma. The painting is bleeding! (*Wrests the gun from her grasp and exits in the same direction as Lord Edgar.*) Lord Edgar!

JANE. (*Calling after him*) Down past the mill run and out onto the moors. The other way, Nicodemus! The other way! Take the short cut through the cedar grove. Faster. Faster, Nicodemus! Faster!

LADY ENID. (*Enters slowly*) Where is Lord Edgar?

JANE. He's searching the moors. He thinks he's seen Victor.

LADY ENID. The wolf or the boy?

JANE. Both.

(*Blackout.*)

SCENE 3

It is nearly dawn of the same night. Lady Enid sits in a chair by the fire, Lord Edgar hovering near her.

LORD EDGAR. Can you tell me how it happened, Enid dearest?

LADY ENID. Jane and I sat up late, she regaling me with tales of Mandacrest, its history, legends and such. As the hour grew late I prepared myself for bed as is my wont. When I had completed my beauty ritual I went straight to our bedchamber and discovered that you had fallen asleep over a book. I crawled in beside you. But unable to sleep myself got up again and came downstairs. As there were some embers of the fire still aglow, I instructed Jane to leave the light when she went to bed, which she did. Then I sat in that chair and began reading your treatise on Lycanthropy and the Dynasties of Egypt. There was a light rain as you will recall. Then it turned to hail. And as I read I listened to the patter of the hailstones on the window panes. It was during that chapter on how the priests of Egypt perfected the art of mummification to the point that the Princess Pev Amri was preserved in a state of suspended animation and was known as She who Sleeps...

LORD EDGAR. But will one day wake.

LADY ENID. Yes, that's it! She Who Sleeps but Will One Day Wake. And how her tomb was guarded by Anubis the Jackal-headed God. But that her tomb has never been found.

LORD EDGAR. That is what is generally believed.

LADY ENID. Then suddenly the pattering at the window caught my attention, for the hail had stopped but the pattering went on. The glass shattered. I turned. It was in the room. I think I screamed. But I couldn't run away! I couldn't run away! It caught me by the hair and then...I can tell no more! I can tell no more!

LORD EDGAR. You seem to have hurt your neck. There is a wound there.

LADY ENID. Wound?!! I feel so weak. I feel so faint. As though I had almost bled to death.

LORD EDGAR. But you couldn't have bled very much. There were no more than five little drops of blood on your dressing gown. Now you'd better get some sleep.

LADY ENID. No sleep! No sleep for me! I shall never sleep again! Sleep is dead. Sleep is dead. She hath murthered sleep. I dare not be alone to sleep. Don't leave me alone. Don't ever leave me alone again. For sleep is dead. Sleep is dead. (*Off*) Who murthered sleep?

LORD EDGAR. Jane will sit with you. (*Leans out the door and speaks to Jane off.*) Take care of her Jane.

(*Enter Nicodemus from French doors.*)

NICODEMUS. Is Lady Enid alive?

LORD EDGAR. She is weak and will sleep long. (*Sighs.*)

NICODEMUS. You sigh . . . Some fearful thoughts, I fear, oppress your heart.

LORD EDGAR. Hush. Hush. She may overhear.

NICODEMUS. Lord Edgar, look at that portrait.

LORD EDGAR. Why, that's blood, isn't it?

NICODEMUS. You must muse upon it.

LORD EDGAR. No, no. I do wish, and yet I dread . . .

NICODEMUS. What?

LORD EDGAR. To say something to you all. But not here — not now — tomorrow.

NICODEMUS. The daylight is coming quickly on.

LORD EDGAR. I will sit up until sunrise. You can fetch my powder-flask and bullets. And if you please, reload the pistols.

NICODEMUS. Lady Enid is alright, I presume.

LORD EDGAR. Yes, but her mind appears to be much disturbed.

NICODEMUS. From bodily weakness, I daresay.

LORD EDGAR. But why should she be bodily weak? She was strong and well but a few hours ago. The glow of youth and health was on her cheeks. Is it possible that she

should become bodily weak in a single night? Nicodemus, sit down. You know that I am not a superstitious
man.

NICODEMUS. You certainly are not.

LORD EDGAR. And yet I have never been so absolutely
staggered as I am by the occurrences of this night.

NICODEMUS. Say on.

LORD EDGAR. I have a frightful, a hideous suspicion
which I fear to mention to anyone lest it be laughed to
scorn.

NICODEMUS. I am lost in wonder.

LORD EDGAR. Nicodemus, swear to me that you will
never repeat to anyone the dreadful suggestion I am
about to make.

NICODEMUS. I swear.

LORD EDGAR. Nicodemus, you have heard of the
dreadful superstition which, in some countries, is ex-
tremely rife, wherein it is believed that there are beings
who never die.

NICODEMUS. Never die?

LORD EDGAR. In a word you have heard of a — heard
of a — oh God in Heaven! I dread to pronounce the
word, though I heard you speak it not three hours past.
Dare I say? . . . Dare I say? . . .

NICODEMUS. Vampire?

LORD EDGAR. You have said it. You have said it.
Nosferatu. But swear to me once more that you will not
repeat it to anyone.

NICODEMUS. Be assured I shall not. I am far from
wishing to keep up in anyone's mind suspicions which I
would fain, very fain refute.

LORD EDGAR. Then let me confide the worst of my
fears Nicodemus.

NICODEMUS. Speak it. Let me hear.

LORD EDGAR. I believe the vampire . . . is one of us.

NICODEMUS. (*Uttering a groan of almost exquisite anguish*) One of us? Oh God! Oh God! Do not too readily yield belief to so dreadful a supposition, I pray you.

LORD EDGAR. Nicodemus, within a fortnight I shall embark for Cairo, there I will organize an expedition to Giza, and certain obscure Numidian ruins in the south.

NICODEMUS. Are you taking Lady Enid?

LORD EDGAR. No, I fear that in her delicate mental state the trip might be too much for her. I will arrange for her to rest in a private sanitarium. Look after Mandacrest until I return. I believe the desert holds some secret. I feel it calling to me. I believe I shall find some answer out there among its pyramids and sacred mummies. At least I know I shall be far away from her.

NICODEMUS. From Lady Enid?

LORD EDGAR. No, from Lady Irma. For Nicodemus it is she I believe has extended her life by feasting on human gore.

NICODEMUS. Say not so!

LORD EDGAR. Irma could never accept the idea of death and decay. She was always seeking consolation in the study of spiritualism and reincarnation. After a while it became an obsession with her. Even on her deathbed she swore she would come back.

NICODEMUS. Do you think she will come again?

LORD EDGAR. I know not. But I almost hope she may. For I would fain speak to her.

NICODEMUS. It is said that if one burns a love letter from a lover who has died at the third crowing of the cock on Saint Swithin's day, you will see the lover ever so briefly.

LORD EDGAR. More superstition.

NICODEMUS. Very like. Very like. Yet after the occurrences of this night I can scarcely distinguish truth from fancy. (*Cock crows off*) There's the cock. 'Twill soon be dawn. Damned spirits all, that in cross ways and floods have burial, already to their wormy beds have gone, for fear lest day should look their shames upon.

LORD EDGAR. (*Amazed*) Nicodemus, you know your Shakespeare!

NICODEMUS. I paraphrase. (*Exits*)

(*The cock crows again.*)

LORD EDGAR. The second crowing of the cock. (*Takes out letters bound with a ribbon*) Irma's letters. Of course it's ridiculous . . . but what harm can it do? I'd best part with them anyway. (*Quotes*) In all the world. In all the world. One thing I know to be true. You'd best be off with the old love before you're on with the new.

(*Burns letter before painting. Cock crows. Painting flies out. A woman's face appears in the painting. She screams.*)

LORD EDGAR. Irma!

Curtain

ACT II

Various places in Egypt.

LORD EDGAR. Ah Egypt! It looks exactly as I pictured it!

ALCAZAR. Osiris hear you!

LORD EDGAR. This invocation is certainly permissible opposite the ancient Diospolis Magna. But we have failed so often. The treasure seekers have always been ahead of us.

ALCAZAR. In recent years our work has been made doubly difficult by the activities of certain political groups seeking to halt the flow of antiquities from out of the country. These armed bandits use this high moral purpose to seize any and all treasures. And this, after the excavators have spent a great deal of time and money to unearth these precious objects, the existence and whereabouts of which these scum were totally unaware.

LORD EDGAR. If we can but find an untouched tomb that can yield up to us its treasures inviolate!

ALCAZAR. I can spare you the disappointments of places I know to be quite empty because the contents have been removed and sold for a good price long ago. I believe I can take you to a syrinx that has never been discovered by the miserable little jackals who take it into their heads to scratch among the tombs.

LORD EDGAR. The idea fascinates me. But to excavate an unopened tomb—not to mention the difficulties of locating one—would require manpower and organizational abilities almost equal to those the Pharaohs employed to seal it.

ALCAZAR. I can place at your disposal a hundred intrepid fellahs, who, incited by baksheesh and a whip of hippopotamus hide would dig down into the bowels of the earth with their fingernails. We might tempt them to bring to light some buried sphinx, to clear away the obstructions before a temple, to open a tomb . . .

LORD EDGAR. (*Smiles dubiously*) Hmmm.

ALCAZAR. I perceive that you are not a mere tourist and · that commonplace curiosities would have no charm for you. So I shall show you a tomb that has escaped the treasure seekers. Long it has lain unknown to any but myself. It is a prize I have guarded for one who should prove worthy of it.

LORD EDGAR. And for which you will make me pay a round sum.

ALCAZAR. I will not deny that I hope to make money. I unearth pharaohs and sell them to people. Pharaohs are getting scarce these days. The article is in demand and it is no longer manufactured.

LORD EDGAR. Let's not beat about the bush. How much do you want?

ALCAZAR. For a tomb that no human hand has disturbed since the priests rolled the rocks before the entrance three thousand years ago, would it be too much to ask a thousand guineas?

LORD EDGAR. A thousand guineas!

ALCAZAR. A mere nothing. After all, the tomb may contain gold in the lump, necklaces of pearls and diamonds, earrings of carbuncle formed from the urine of lynxes, sapphire seals, ancient idols of precious metals; why, the currency of the time, that by itself would bring a good price.

LORD EDGAR. (*Aside*) Artful scoundrel! He knows perfectly well that such things are not to be found in Egyptian sepulchres.

ALCAZAR. Well, my lord, does the bargain suit you?

LORD EDGAR. Yes, we will call it a thousand guineas. If the tomb has never been touched and nothing — not even a stone — has been disturbed by the levers of the excavators; and on condition that we can carry everything away.

ALCAZAR. I accept. You can risk the bank notes and gold without fear. It seems your prayer has been answered.

LORD EDGAR. Perhaps we are rejoicing too soon and are about to experience the same disappointments encountered by Belzoni when he believed he was the first to enter the tomb of Menepha Seti. He, after having passed through a maze of corridors, pits, and chambers, found only an empty sarcophagus with a broken lid, for the treasure-seekers had attained the royal tomb by mining through the rocks from the other direction.

ALCAZAR. Oh no! This tomb is too far removed for those accursed moles to have found their way there. I have lived many years in the valley of the kings and my eyes have become as piercing as those of the sacred hawks perched on the entablatures of the temples. For years I have not so much as dared to cast a glance in that direction, fearing to arouse the suspicions of the violators of the tombs. This way, my lord. (*They exit*)

(*The lights fade and come up somewhere in the tomb. It is very dark. From time to time some detail emerges from the darkness in the light of their lanterns.*)

LORD EDGAR. The deuce! Are we going down to the center of the earth? The heat increases to such a degree that we cannot be far from the infernal regions.

ALCAZAR. It is a pit, Milord. What's to be done?

LORD EDGAR. We must lower ourselves on ropes. (*Echo*) These cursed Egyptians were so cunning about hiding the entrances of their burial burrows. They could not think of enough ways to puzzle poor people. One can imagine them laughing beforehand at the downcast faces of the excavators.

ALCAZAR. Another dead end.

LORD EDGAR. It looks like they've beaten us this round. Rap on the floor and listen for a hollow sound. (*They do so. After much rapping the wall gives back a hollow sound.*)

LORD EDGAR. Help me to remove this block. It's a bit low. We'll have to crawl on our faces.

ALCAZAR. Oy!

(*They do so.*)

ALCAZAR. Look there, Milord.

LORD EDGAR. The familiar personages of the psychostasia with Osiris as judge. (*Stands*) Well well, my dear Alcazar. So far you have kept your part of the bargain. We are indeed the first human beings who have entered here since the dead, whoever he may be, was abandoned to eternity and oblivion in the tomb.

ALCAZAR. Oh, he must have been a very powerful personage—a prince of the royal household at least.

LORD EDGAR. I will tell you after I decipher his cartouche.

ALCAZAR. But first let us enter the most beautiful room of all, the room the ancient Egyptians called The Golden Room.

LORD EDGAR. Really, I have some compunction of conscience about disturbing the last rest of this poor unknown mortal who felt so sure that he would rest in peace until the end of the world. Our visit will be a most unwelcome one to the host of this mansion.

ALCAZAR. You'll be wanting a proper introduction and I have lived long enough among the Pharaohs to make you one. I know how to present you to the illustrious inhabitant of this subterranean palace.

LORD EDGAR. Look, a five-toed footprint in the dust.

ALCAZAR. Footprint?

LORD EDGAR. It looks as though it were made yesterday.

ALCAZAR. How can that be?

LORD EDGAR. It must have been the last footprint made by the last slave leaving the burial chamber thirty-five hundred years ago. There has not been a breath of air in here to disturb it. Why, mighty civilizations have risen and fallen since this footprint was made. Their pomp, their power, their monuments of stone have not lasted as long as this insignificant footprint in the dust.

(*Sarcophagus revealed.*)

ALCAZAR. My lord! My lord! The sarcophagus is intact!

LORD EDGAR. Is it possible, my dear Alcazar — is it intact? (*Examines the sarcophagus then exclaims rapturously*) Incredible good fortune! Marvelous chance! Priceless treasure!

ALCAZAR. (*Aside*) I asked too little. This my lord has robbed me.

LORD EDGAR. There there, Alcazar. A bargain is a bargain. Here are the vases that held the viscera of the mummy contained in the sarcophagus. Nothing has been touched in this palace of death since the day when the mummy, in its coffins and cerements, had been laid upon its couch of basalt.

ALCAZAR. Observe that these are not the usual funerary offerings.

LORD EDGAR. Don't touch it! Touch nothing! It might crumble. First I must decipher this cartouche. "She Who Sleeps but Will One Day Wake." A lotus sarcophagus. Hmmmm. Notice that the lotus motif recurs as well as the Ankh, emblem of eternal life. Must you smoke those nasty musk-scented cigarettes? There's little enough air in here as it is.

LORD EDGAR. Certainly. But take care not to injure the lid when opening it, for I want to remove this monument and make a present of it to the British Museum.

(*They remove the cover.*)

ALCAZAR. A woman! A woman!

LORD EDGAR. Astonishing novelty! The necropolis of the queens is situated farther off, in a gorge of the mountains. The tombs of the queens are very simple. Let me decipher the cartouche. "She who sleeps but will one day wake."

ALCAZAR. (*Pointing to the butt*) This is a very primitive heiroglyph.

LORD EDGAR. It's a little behind.

ALCAZAR. It's almost more than I can believe.

LORD EDGAR. It's *altogether* more than *I* can believe.

ALCAZAR. What? You see these things before your very eyes and still you do not believe.

LORD EDGAR. The women of the East have always been considered inferior to the men even after death. The greater part of these tombs, violated at very remote epochs, have served as receptacles for deformed mummies, rudely embalmed, that still exhibit traces of leprosy and elephantiasis. By what means, by what miracle of substitution, had this woman's coffin found its way into this royal sarcophagus, in the midst of this palatial crypt, worthy of the most illustrious and powerful of the

Pharaohs? This unsettles all of my opinions and theories and contradicts the most reliable authorities on the subject of the Egyptian funeral rites so uniform in every respect for thousands of years.

ALCAZAR. We have no doubt alighted on some mystery, some obscure point lost to history. Had some ambitious woman usurped the tomb as she had the throne?

LORD EDGAR. What a charming custom. To bury a young woman with all the coquettish arsenal of her toilette about her. For there can be no doubt that it is a young woman enveloped in these bands of linen stained yellow with age and essences.

ALCAZAR. Compared with the ancient Egyptians we are veritable barbarians: dragging out a mere animal existence. We no longer have any delicacy of sentiment connected with death. What tenderness, what regret, what love, are revealed in this devoted attention, this unlimited precaution, this vain solicitude that no one would ever witness, the affection lavished upon an insensible corpse, these efforts to snatch from destruction an adored form, and to present it to the soul intact upon the great day of the resurrection.

LORD EDGAR. Someday we may attain to such heights of civilization and refinement of feeling. In the meantime let us disrobe this young beauty, more than three thousand years old, with all the delicacy possible.

ALCAZAR. Poor lady, profane eyes are about to rest upon charms unknown to love itself, perhaps.

LORD EDGAR. Strange. I feel embarrassed at not having the proper costume in which to present myself before a royal mummy.

ALCAZAR. There is no time here. In this tomb, far away from the banal stupidities of the modern world, we might just as well be in ancient Egypt on the day this cherished being was entrusted to eternity.

(*They unwrap the mummy's hand which holds a scroll.*)

LORD EDGAR. Extraordinary! In most cases the mummification is accomplished through the use of bitumen and natron. Here, the body, prepared by a longer, safer and more costly process has preserved the elasticity of the flesh, the grain of the epidermis, and a color that is almost natural. The skin has the fine hue of a new Florentine bronze and the warm amber tint of a Titian.

ALCAZAR. By the knees of Amon Ra—behold—there is a scroll clasped in her hand!

LORD EDGAR. (*Gently unrolls the scroll*) Bring that electric torch here. "She who sleeps but will one day wake." It is the same cartouche unmistakably. (*Reads on silently, then mutters.*) Good God! It can't be! It can't be!

ALCAZAR. What does it say?

LORD EDGAR. (*Awed*) It is the formula to revive the princess. To return her to life once more.

ALCAZAR. But surely you don't . . .

LORD EDGAR. It's more than I can believe at the moment, Alcazar. But something inside me wants to believe. (*He reads more.*) Well! This is simple enough. These caskets and bottles and bowls contain the ingredients in the formula. (*Reads*) The priest must wear certain vestments and douse the lid with wine. The wine in these bottles has dried up over the centuries. Oh drat! I have no wine. I am an abstainer.

ALCAZAR. (*Produces a bottle of wine from his pocket*) I have wine. Very good wine. And although it is a madeira, of somewhat more recent vintage, I believe it may suffice. The wine may very well be the least important element in the formula.

LORD EDGAR. (*Reads*) It says here that the priest must be alone with the mummy when the soul is called back from the underworld.

ALCAZAR. Permit me to withdraw and leave you alone with your newfound lady friend. But before I go, may I make one request?

LORD EDGAR. Certainly, Alcazar, what is it?

ALCAZAR. Leave some wine for the return trip.

LORD EDGAR. I'll use only what is absolutely necessary to complete the ritual.

ALCAZAR. Thank you. (*Exits backwards making a salaam as he goes out.*)

LORD EDGAR. (*Dresses himself in the costume of the Egyptian priest. Lights the charcoal braziers in the perfuming pans on either side of the sarcophagus. And intones the following invocation*) Katara katara katara rana! Ecbatana Ecbatana Soumouft! Soumouft! Fahata fahata Habebe! Oh Habebe! Oh Habebe! Habebe tay! (*He gently unwraps the mummy as the music swells.*)

PEV AMRI. (*Flutters her eyelashes and opens her eyes*) Habebe? Habebe tay?

LORD EDGAR. (*Cries out*) Oh God!

PEV AMRI. (*Dances, then*) Fahouta bala bala mem fou ha ram sahadi Karnak!

LORD EDGAR. Oh exquisite! Exquisite beauty!

PEV AMRI. Han fu bazaar danbazaar.

LORD EDGAR. Forgive me divine one, but your spoken language is lost on me.

PEV AMRI. Mabouka. Giza. (*Laughs, then looking into Sarcophagus and touching herself*) Ankh! Ankh!

LORD EDGAR. (*Exclaims*) Ankh! Life! Ankh! Life! Life!

PEV AMRI. Ankh . . . life?

LORD EDGAR. Ankh . . . life.

PEV AMRI. Life. Life!

LORD EDGAR. Life!

PEV AMRI. (*Writhing, indicates stiffness of spine.*) Cairo! Cairo! Practor! [(*If audience hisses*) Asp!] (*Gestures, pointing to mouth.*)

LORD EDGAR. Those lips. Silent for three thousand years now beg to be kissed. But do I dare? (*Kisses her.*)

PEV AMRI. (*She slaps him*) Puna kha fo ha na ba bhouna. (*Makes gesture that she is hungry.*) Bhouna! Bhouna!

LORD EDGAR. Hungry? Of course you must be hungry after not having eaten in three millennia. I'll get you food. A loaf of bread, a jug of wine, a book of verse and thou beside me in the wilderness and wilderness is paradise enow! (*Kisses her hand.*)

PEV AMRI. Amon! Amon Ra! Ahmin-hotep. Memphis. Geza. Aswan. Hatshepsut. Toot 'n come in! (*Sniffs*) Sphinx! (*Scurries back into the mummy case, closes the door after her*)

(*Lord Edgar runs out to get Alcazar.*)

PEV AMRI. (*Scurries back into the mummy case, sniffs*) Sphinx!

(*Closes the door after her.*)

LORD EDGAR. (*Off*) Alcazar! Alcazar! She's hungry! She wants food!

ALCAZAR. (*Off*) She wants? Surely you don't mean . . .

LORD EDGAR. Yes it's true! It's true! She's alive! She's alive. In flesh and blood.

ALCAZAR. My boy you have stayed too long in the tomb. Your mind is playing tricks on you.

LORD EDGAR. Come if you don't believe me. See for yourself. (*He rushes onto the stage. Alcazar follows behind somewhat slowly and dubiously. He is obviously totally unconvinced.*) Where is she? She's gone. . . . She was here a minute ago.

ALCAZAR. Akh—naten!

LORD EDGAR. I tell you she spoke! I kissed those divine lips. Look! She gave me this ring!

ALCAZAR. We must leave before dawn. If they find us looting the tomb they will report us to the authorities.

LORD EDGAR. But she's alive, I tell you, alive! (*Calling*) Princess! Princess, where are you? Where are you, Pev Amri? Pev!

(*Inside the sarcophagus stands a mummy as before, only this time the wrappings have been partially removed revealing a hideously decomposed face through the dried flesh of which the skull protrudes.*)

LORD EDGAR. (*Screams*) No! It can't be! It can't be! Pev. Pev. I should never have summoned you, Alcazar. It broke the spell and sent her back to the underworld.

ALCAZAR. The hour grows late. We must leave before dawn. Pack up whatever you want to take along.

LORD EDGAR. I must take her with me. I must find a way to bring her back again. If it's the last thing I do, I'll bring her back again!

ALCAZAR. Let us remove the sarcophagus. The most dangerous part is over. Rain is what we have to fear now.

(*They carry out the mummy case. Lights fade.*)

ACT III

Scene 1

The scene is Mandacrest. The time is Autumn. Jane is dusting the mummy case. Nicodemus looks on.

NICODEMUS. It was a devil of a time we had getting it in here. The thing must weigh a ton.

JANE. Did you bring Lady Enid's trunk upstairs?

NICODEMUS. Yes.

JANE. Where is she?

NICODEMUS. Alone with her secrets: old feather fans, tasselled dance cards, powdered with musk, a gaud of amber beads locked away in her drawer. A program from Antoine's when she appeared with Bonita Bainbridge in *The Farfelu of Seville.*

JANE. It's the paralysis of the insane. She sleeps all day and she's up all night.

NICODEMUS. That was always her way.

JANE. She's got terrible insomnia.

NICODEMUS. Can't remember a thing, eh?

JANE. And when she's up — she walks.

NICODEMUS. And why shouldn't she walk? It's daft she is, not crippled.

JANE. I haven't slept a wink since they brought her home a week ago.

NICODEMUS. You're doing the work of three people.

JANE. I asked Lord Edgar if I could get a slight raise in pay and he said he'd consider it.

NICODEMUS. And to think of you having to beg from these swine. I'm the only one who knows what you are. Why don't you trust me more? What have you got up your nose against me?

JANE. (*Crosses to the mirror*) Come to the glass, Nicodemus, and I'll show you what you should wish. Do you

47

mark those two lines between your eyes? And those thick brows that instead of rising, arched, sink in the middle? And that couple of black fiends, so deeply buried, who never open their windows boldly, but lurk glinting under them, like devil's spies? Wish and learn to smooth away the surly wrinkles, to raise your lids frankly, and change the fiends to confident, innocent angels, suspecting and doubting nothing, and always seeing friends where they are not sure of foes. Don't get the expression of a vicious cur that appears to know the kicks it gets are its dessert, and yet hates all the world, as well as the kicker, for what it suffers.

NICODEMUS. In other words, I must wish for Edgar Hillcrest's great blue eyes and even forehead. I do, but that won't help me to them. I was abandoned. Found on the doorstep of a London doss house. My own mother didn't want me.

JANE. Who knows but your father was emperor of China and your mother was an Indian queen, each of them able to buy up Mandacrest with one week's income. And you were kidnapped by wicked sailors and brought to England. Were I in your place, I would frame high notions of my birth, and the thoughts of what I was should give me courage and dignity.

NICODEMUS. Thank you, Janey. In the future while I'm shovelling shit I'll try to think of myself as a prince in disguise.

JANE. (*Looking out of the door-windows*) Why don't you do some washin' and combin' and go to the village and visit that dairy maid you've taken a fancy to.

NICODEMUS. She's a cute little baggage but she smells of cheese.

JANE. It's a good night for wooing for the moon is full. (*Bell off*) There's the bell. The mistress wants me. (*Exits*)

NICODEMUS. The moon is full? (*Goes upstage and*

looks out through the doors) A full moon. (*He begins to make jerky movements*) A full moooooon!
howl as Nicodemus with his back to the audience raises one arm, which has become a wolf's paw) No! No! No! Oh God! God help me! Don't let it happen! It's the moooooon! Moooooooooon! (*He turns to the audience. His face has become that of a wolf. He runs about the stage on his tiptoes with his knees bent. He sniffs, scratches, lifts his leg against a piece of furniture, howls and runs out.*)

JANE. (*Enters*) Nicodemus, Lady Enid wants to have a word with you. (*Sees the door left open*) He's gone and he's left the door wide open again. God, he'll never change.

(*There is the sound of a wolf howling in the distance.*)

LADY ENID. (*Enters*) Do you hear that? First you think it's a wolf. Then you tell yourself it's the wind. But you know that it's a soul in pain. (*Crosses to the fireplace*) Get that flower out of here!

JANE. I thought it looked so lovely.

LADY ENID. I can stand neither its color nor its scent. Take it away.

JANE. It's the last rose of summer. (*Exits with vase*)

(*LADY ENID takes down a dulcimer, lays it across her lap, and begins to play "The Last Rose of Summer." Jane returns with another dulcimer. She sits on the other side of the fireplace and joins Lady Enid in a duet.*)

LADY ENID. (*Staring at the portrait over the mantel*) Who is that woman?

JANE. Why that's yourself, Lady Enid.

LADY ENID. No, no, that's not me. She's a virgin.

JANE. It was painted a long time ago.

LADY ENID. She still has her illusions. She still has her faith. No, that isn't me.

JANE. Virginity is the balloon in the carnival of life. It vanishes with the first prick.

LADY ENID. (*Stops playing abruptly*) In all of England I don't believe I could have married into a situation so completely removed from the stir of society. A perfect misanthropist's heaven: and Lord Edgar and I are such a perfect pair to divide the desolation between us.

JANE. It's a refuge, it is, from the chatter of tongues.

LADY ENID. Mine eyes itch. Doth that bode weeping?

JANE. Maybe you've got something in your eye, Lady Enid.

LADY ENID. Where is Nicodemus? I want to have a word with him.

JANE. I'm afraid that's not possible Lady Enid.

LADY ENID. And why not? Send for Nicodemus. I demand to see him at once.

JANE. Nicodemus can't come, Lady Enid. For obvious reasons.

LADY ENID. Obvious reasons? (*The light dawns.*) Oh! Oh! For obvious reasons. Oh I see. In that case, I'll go to him.

JANE. Are you fond of Nicodemus?

LADY ENID. Fond of Nicodemus? Sometimes I feel that I am Nicodemus. That Nicodemus and I are one and the same person.

JANE. Now now, Lady Enid, what have you got up your sleeve?

LADY ENID. Up my sleeve? Up my sleeve? (*She looks up her sleeve. Her own hand comes out in a claw-like gesture. She screams.*)

JANE. Don't be frightened, Lady Enid. That's your own hand.

LADY ENID. I frighten myself sometimes. Jane, I fear that Lord Edgar and I are drifting apart. It's a terrible thing to marry an Egyptologist and find out he's hung up on his mummy. [(*If audience hisses.*) *That wind!*]

JANE. He's an incurable romantic. If you really want to please him, you should try to appeal to that side of his nature. I have a lovely old dress you could wear. It's a family heirloom. It's full of nostalgia.

LADY ENID. We could have it cleaned.

JANE. I'll lay it out in your room. Wear it tonight. It's sure to get a strong reaction.

LADY ENID. Thank you, Jane.

(*Exit Jane. Lady Enid picks up dulcimer, plays "Skip to My Lou." Lord Edgar enters.*)

LADY ENID. Edgar darling, where have you been?

LORD EDGAR. I've been to the jewelers.

LADY ENID. To buy jewelry?

LORD EDGAR. No, bullets. Silver bullets. The young dairy maid in the village was found badly mauled. It seems the werewolf has struck again. I must go to the morgue.

LADY ENID. Oh Edgar. Why don't you just go and live at the morgue instead of making a morgue of our home. (*She flings out.*)

LORD EDGAR. (*Calling after her*) Enid. Enid darling. Please be reasonable.

(*Nicodemus appears in the French doors Up. He has blood on his hand.*)

NICODEMUS. Lord Edgar.

LORD EDGAR. Nicodemus. I'll be needing your help tonight. The werewolf has struck again. This time, the cur must die.

NICODEMUS. Must he die? Is there no other help for him? Can't he be put away somewhere where he could receive therapy? Perhaps some day, science will discover a cure for what he has.

LORD EDGAR. There is only one cure for what he has. The barrel of a gun and a silver bullet. (*Lord Edgar exits.*)

NICODEMUS. Oh miserable me. Must I, like Tancred in *Jerusalem Delivered*, ever injure what I love beyond all else? Unloved I lived. Unloved I die. My only crime was having been born.

(*Enter Jane.*)

JANE. And who are you talking to, Nicodemus Underwood.

NICODEMUS. Myself. The only one who'll listen.

JANE. Did you see the milkmaid tonight, Nicodemus?

NICODEMUS. The milkmaid, oh, the milkmaid. Would that I had never seen the milkmaid.

JANE. There's blood on your hand. Did you hurt yourself?

NICODEMUS. No. It's her blood. The blood of the tender maid you spoke of. The werewolf got her.

JANE. Werewolf?

NICODEMUS. Yes, you know, a person who dons the skin of a wolf in the full of the moon and turns into a wolf to prowl at night. A woman is usually the victim. It makes a horrible story.

JANE. And where is it now, this hound of hell?

NICODEMUS. Wipe from my hand the blood you see with your dainty little hankie, and behold the mark of Cain.

NICODEMUS. Wipe the blood from my palm with your dainty little hankie, and see the mark of Cain.

JANE. (*Spits on her hankie and wipes some of the blood from Nicodemus' palm. She gasps and jumps back.*) The Pentagram! When did this happen to you?

NICODEMUS. Tonight, in the full of the moon! I turned into a wolf! And took the life of the only fair creature who'd ever shown me any love.

JANE. But the moon is still full. How come you're not a wolf now?

NICODEMUS. I'm in remission since a cloud passed over the moon.

JANE. Unspeakable horror!

NICODEMUS. Unspeakable shame! For I fear what I may do next. For it is the thing I love I kill. And I love you Janey, with all my heart.

JANE. No you don't. It's just infatuation tinged with lust.

NICODEMUS. And I love Lady Enid.

JANE. Lady Enid?

NICODEMUS. Yes. I'd have never dared confess it until this moment. But now I fear I may be some danger to her person. All must out!

JANE. Run away, Nicodemus. Run away and never come back!

NICODEMUS. Where shall I go? I've never known any life but Mandacrest! I have no money, no luggage!

JANE. Go upstairs to my room. On the table by my bed you will find a copy of Lord Lytton's Zanoni. In it I have saved a few pounds. Take them. You may need them.

NICODEMUS. Thank you, Janey. (*Exits*)

JANE. Sufficient unto the night are the horrors thereof. (*Falls on knees and prays*) Please God, don't let anything happen to Lord Edgar, don't let anything happen to Lady Enid, and please God, don't let anything happen to me!

LADY ENID. (*Enters in a different frock*) How do I look?

JANE. Lovely, Lady Enid. It's sure to put Lord Edgar into a romantic mood. This dress was always his favorite.

LADY ENID. Are you sure he really likes it?

JANE. Positive. He's even worn it himself when in an antic mood, in younger, happier days. (*Exit Jane.*)

LADY ENID. (*Goes over to the mantel and looks up at the portrait*) Well any man who dresses up as a woman can't be all bad! (*To herself in the portrait*) If you continue at this rate you'll be an even greater actress than Bonita Bainbridge!

VOICE. (*Off left, moans twice, then*) Help me. Help me! Turn the figurine. Turn the figurine!

(*Lady Enid moves an ornament on the fireplace, triggering a sliding panel. The bookcase slides back, revealing a cage. She jumps back, startled. A shrouded figure appears within the cage.*)

LADY ENID. Who are you? What are you doing in there?

VOICE. They keep me here! I'm their prisoner! They torture me! Please help me! Help me!

LADY ENID. Who? Who tortures you?

VOICE. Edgar! Edgar tortures me!

LADY ENID. You poor thing. Who are you?

VOICE. Why, I'm his wife, Irma.

LADY ENID. Irma!

VOICE. Irma Vep! The first Lady Hillcrest.

LADY ENID. But I thought you were dead!

IRMA. That's what they want you to think! That's what they want everyone to think!

LADY ENID. Why have they put you here?

IRMA. There are jewels hidden in the house. I alone know where they are. But I'll never tell! For if I tell, they'll kill me! If you help me, I'll tell you where the jewels are, and I'll share them with you.

LADY ENID. Poor woman! Of course I'll help you. But this cage is locked!

IRMA. Jane has the key! Steal it from her! But don't tell her you've seen me! Don't tell anyone! Not Jane. Not Nicodemus! Not Lord Edgar! (*Footsteps are heard*) I hear someone coming. Turn the figurine! And please, please remember me! Remember me!

LADY ENID. Remember you? Of course I'll remember you! How could I forget you. You poor darling. Poor, poor darling! (*Turns the figurine. The bookcase starts to close and sticks. Enid struggles with the figurine. The bookcase closes fully as Lord Edgar enters.*)

LORD EDGAR. Enid!

LADY ENID. (*Turning*) Edgar.

LORD EDGAR. Where did you get that dress?

LADY ENID. Do you like it?

LORD EDGAR. Like it? I hate it! I despise it! I loathe it! Take it off! Take it off!

LADY ENID. But Edgar! I only wanted to please you!

LORD EDGAR. Please me? You wanted to torture me! You wanted to make me suffer! I'll never forgive you for this Enid. Never!

LADY ENID. But Edgar! I only wanted to be nearer to you!

LORD EDGAR. You've only driven me further away. I'd rather see you locked away in rags in the deepest darkest dungeon I could find than see you in that dress!

LADY ENID. No!

LORD EDGAR. Take it off, I said! You're making me hate you!

LADY ENID. What are you saying?

LORD EDGAR. It was her dress.

LADY ENID. *Her* dress?

LORD EDGAR. Irma's!

LADY ENID. Jane didn't tell me that!

LORD EDGAR. Jane told you to wear that? She should have known better. She knows how it upsets me to see the dress Irma wore the night she died!

LADY ENID. Died? But she . . . she didn't . . .

LORD EDGAR. Didn't what?

LADY ENID. (*Catching herself*)   . . die in this dress, did she?

LORD EDGAR. Oh don't talk about it anymore! You'll only make me hate you more. (*Tears her dress. Lady Enid bursts into tears and runs to the door.*) Stop, Enid! I'm sorry. I didn't mean it.

LADY ENID. You don't love me and you never have.

LORD EDGAR. You're wrong! I love no one else but you.

LADY ENID. Then why, why, why must we go on living here as brother and sister? Why can't you live with me as a wife?

LORD EDGAR. Because of the terror I feel of *her* . . .

LADY ENID. Terror?

LORD EDGAR. Yes, terror! Terror! A terror so great that I've never been able to communicate it to anyone.

LADY ENID. Even your wife?

LORD EDGAR. Very well, then, I'll tell you. Sometimes I see her standing before me as big as life.

LADY ENID. How does she look?

LORD EDGAR. Oh, very well. Exactly as she did when I saw her last, three years ago.

LADY ENID. Three years ago?

LORD EDGAR. She won't let me go. I'm her prisoner.

LADY ENID. *She* won't let *you* go?

LORD EDGAR. Yes, yes, she's horrible. I'll never get rid of her.

LADY ENID. But you have gotten rid of her. On your trip to Egypt. You said you'd found something in the tomb that had made you forget all about her.

LORD EDGAR. Don't talk about it. Or think of it, even. There was no help for me there. I can feel it in my bones. I didn't get rid of it out there either.

LADY ENID. Of what? What do you mean?

LORD EDGAR. I mean the horror. The fantastic hold on my mind, on my soul.

LADY ENID. But you said it was over.

LORD EDGAR. No no, that's just the thing. It isn't.

LADY ENID. Not over?

LORD EDGAR. No Enid, it's not over, and I'm afraid it never will be.

LADY ENID. (*In a strangled voice*) Are you saying then that in your heart of hearts you'll never be able to forget this woman?

LORD EDGAR. She comes toward me, and puts her arms around me. Then she presses her lips to mine.

LADY ENID. To kiss you?

LORD EDGAR. As if to kiss me — but she doesn't kiss. She sucks.

LADY ENID. Sucks?

LORD EDGAR. She sucks my breath until I feel I'm suffocating. (*Turns blue.*)

LADY ENID. Good God! Edgar! You're sick! You're much sicker than you thought. Than either of us thought.

LORD EDGAR. (*Clutching at his throat*) Yes! Yes! I can't breathe! I'm suffocating, and her fingers are tightening! Tightening around my throat. Help me. Help me.

LADY ENID. Oh, my dear Lord Edgar! Then you've been suffering in silence all this time and you've never told me anything about it?

LORD EDGAR. I couldn't tell you. I couldn't speak

the unspeakable—name the unnameable. (*Gasps for breath.*) And her fingers are tightening. Tightening more and more. Help me! Help me!

LADY ENID. Nicodemus! (*Runs Off calling.*) Nicodemus.

NICODEMUS. (*Off*) You called, Lady Enid?

LADY ENID. (*Off*) Yes please, please help me. Lord Edgar is having an attack. (*She weeps.*)

NICODEMUS. (*Off*) There there, Lady Enid. Calm yourself.

LADY ENID. (*Off*) Oh please, hurry, hurry!

NICODEMUS. (*Off*) Stay here. I'll go to him. (*Enters.*) There there, Lord Edgar. Doing poorly? Have you got the horrors again?

LORD EDGAR. (*Rolling about on the floor, clutching his throat*) Yes yes, the horrors. It's her. I'll never be free of her.

NICODEMUS. (*Offering his flask*) Here you go. You must fight fire with fire and spirits with spirits!

LORD EDGAR. No, I won't break my rule. You know I am an abstainer.

NICODEMUS. Oh well then, in that case . . . (*Drinks himself.*)

LORD EDGAR. (*Seeing this*) On second thought, maybe just a drop.

NICODEMUS. (*Passing him the flask*) For medicinal purposes only. (*Lord Edgar drinks*) Feeling better?

LORD EDGAR. Yes, much. Thanks. Nicodemus, stay with Lady Enid tonight.

NICODEMUS. With Lady Enid?

LORD EDGAR. Yes, there's a wolf about, and I don't want her left alone. (*Exits up center.*)

NICODEMUS. No, no, Lord Edgar. Not that! Don't ask me that! Anything but that! Horror. Horror.

Horror. For I fear the gibbous moon. Oh horror! Oh horror!

JANE. (*Enters with wolfbane*) Did you find the money?

NICODEMUS. Yes, thank you Janey.

JANE. Now go, Nicodemus. I've never liked you, but I've never wished you any harm. May God help you!

NICODEMUS. Thank you, Janey. This is the only kindness anyone has ever shown me.

JANE. Ah, be off with you. I have to put up wolfbane against you.

NICODEMUS. I understand. (*Exits*)

(*Jane hangs up wolfbane around the room. Lady Enid enters.*)

LADY ENID. Where's Lord Edgar?

JANE. He's gone out, after the wolf.

LADY ENID. Is he hunting wolves again, with one of his villainous old guns?

JANE. I think he took a horse pistol.

LADY ENID. The blackguard.

JANE. Now Lady Enid, I won't have you talking this way about Lord Edgar.

LADY ENID. (*Seizing her by the wrist*) When a woman loves a man she should be willing to do anything for him. Cut off her little finger at the middle joint there. (*Twisting Jane's finger*)

JANE. (*Loudly*) Ow!

LADY ENID. Or cut off her dainty hand at the wrist.

JANE. Please, let go. You're hurting me!

LADY ENID. Or lop off her pretty little ear.'(*Twists her ear and takes keys.*)

JANE. Ow! Ow! Ow! Please stop!

LADY ENID. When you're willing to do those things for Lord Edgar then entertain thoughts of loving him. Otherwise back off. (*Releases her.*)

JANE. (*Rubbing her wrist*) Now look. You've left red marks on my wrist. You've got a devil in you. That's what it is. You know I'm nothing to Lord Edgar. I have no more hold over his heart than you have. It's Irma he loves! Irma Vep. It's no use our fighting over the same man — when he's in love with a dead woman.

LADY ENID. You scandalous little hypocrite! Are you not afraid of being carried away bodily whenever you mention the devil's name? I warn you to refrain from provoking me or I will ask your abduction as a special favor.

(*Jane goes to leave.*)

LADY ENID. Stop Jane! Look here. I'll show you how far I've progressed in the Black Art. (*Taking down a book from the shelf*) I shall soon be competent to make a clear house of it. The red cow didn't die by chance; and your rheumatism can hardly be reckoned among providential visitations!

JANE. Oh wicked! Wicked! May the Lord deliver us from evil!

LADY ENID. No, reprobate! You are a castaway. Be off, or I'll hurt you seriously. I'll have you all modeled in wax and clay; and the first who passes the limits I fix, shall . . . I'll not say what he shall be done to . . . but you'll see! Go; I'm looking at you.

JANE. (*Trembling with sincere horror, hurries out praying and ejaculating*) Wicked! Wicked!

LADY ENID. (*Laughing*) Wicked, perhaps. But I have the keys! (*She approaches the bookcase. She turns the figurine. The bookcase slides back.*) Psst! Psst! Irma! Irma darling. Are you there?

IRMA. Where else would I be? Did you get the key?

LADY ENID. Yes, I have it.

IRMA. Open the door. Quickly. Quickly!

LADY ENID. But I don't know which one it is.

IRMA. Quickly! Quickly! Before someone comes.

LADY ENID. (*Trying one key after another*) Well there are so many of them.

IRMA. Quickly! Save me! Save me!

LADY ENID. (*Opening the door*) Ah, there, Irma dearest. You're free.

(*Irma flies out of the door shrieking like a madwoman. She seizes Enid by the throat, turns her back to the audience, and leans over her. Enid sinks to her knees.*)

IRMA. (*Calmly*) Oh triple fool! Did you not know that Irma Vep is "vampire" anagrammatized!

LADY ENID. (*Reaches up and rips off Irma's face, which is a rubber mask, revealing the other player.*)

LADY ENID. Edgar?

JANE. No, Jane!

LADY ENID. Jane! You?

JANE. Yes, I did it! I killed the child, and Irma too! I was the vampire, feeding on the lifeblood of my own jealousy! No more will I eat the bitter crust of charity, nor serve a vain mistress!

LADY ENID. You? You killed her?

JANE. Yes I killed her, and I'll kill again. I'd kill any woman who stood in my way.

LADY ENID. You're mad.

JANE. Mad? Mad? (*She laughs maniacally*) Perhaps I am. Love is a kind of madness. And hatred is a bottomless cup, and I will drink the dregs.

(*Jane pulls out a meatcleaver and attacks Enid. Enid, who has backed over to the mummy case, deftly opens the door as Jane runs at her. Jane goes into the*

mummy case. Enid slams the door and holds it shut.
We hear Jane pounding within the mummy case.)

LADY ENID. (*Crying out*) Help me! Nicodemus!
Edgar! Someone! Anyone! Help me!
LORD EDGAR. (*Rushes in*) Enid, what is it?
LADY ENID. (*Hysterically*) She's in the mummy case.
She's in the mummy case. You can hear her rapping.

(*The rapping stops.*)

LORD EDGAR. I don't hear anything.
LADY ENID. I found it all out. Jane killed Irma, and
the child! Irma Vep is "vampire" anagrammatized.
LORD EDGAR. Enid, I think your mind is affected.
LADY ENID. No, it's Jane. Jane is mad. Mad, I tell you.
She attacked me with a meat axe. She's in the mummy
case. Call Scotland Yard.
LORD EDGAR. Nonsense, Enid. (*Goes to open the
mummy case.*)
LADY ENID. What are you going to do?
LORD EDGAR. I'm going to open the mummy case.
LADY ENID. No, don't open the mummy case.
LORD EDGAR. I'm going to open the mummy case.
Stand back.
LADY ENID. Don't open the mummy case.
LORD EDGAR. I'm going to open the mummy case.
LADY ENID. Don't open the mummy case. Don't
open it. Don't open it. Don't . . .
LORD EDGAR. (*Opens the mummy case*) See Enid?
The mummy case is perfectly empty.
LADY ENID. (*Somewhat mollified*) Well, she was in
there a moment ago. (*The lights begin to dim*) The
lights. The lights are dimming. The lights. The lights
are dimming. (*The lights come back up.*)

LORD EDGAR. Nonsense, Enid. The lights are not dimming. Come and sit by the fire.

(*Lights dim again.*)

LADY ENID. The lights are dimming.

LORD EDGAR. (*He escorts her to chair*) If you don't stop, Enid, they'll put you back in the sanitarium and they'll never let you out again.

LADY ENID. (*In a tiny voice*) The lights are dimming.
The lights are not dimming!

LADY ENID. (*In a tiny voice*) The lights are dimming.

LORD EDGAR. (*Infuriated*) Stop it, Enid! Stop it stop it stop it stop it! I don't want to hear you say that again!

LADY ENID. (*Turns to the audience and silently mouths the words "The lights are dimming."*)

LORD EDGAR. There's the good girl. There's the good girl. Go on, play your dulcimer like the good girl. Play with your dulcimer, Enid. (*Crosses to the door to exit*) And I'll have Jane fix you a nice hot cup of tea.

LADY ENID. (*Winces*)

LORD EDGAR. Tch tch tch! (*Exits*)

LADY ENID. (*Begins to play "The Last Rose of Summer" on her dulcimer as ominous music swells*) Is it possible my mind is affected? And yet I saw it with my very eyes. (*There is a tapping at the window, as in Act I.*) There it is again! Oh god. Oh god in heaven. There it is again. The rapping! The rapping! As if someone gently tapping. (*She takes the poker from the fireside and approaches the French doors stealthily and flies through them, brandishing the poker*) Tapping at my chamber door!

NICODEMUS. (*Off*) Hey Lady Enid! What's going on? (*Poking his head through the door*) What's going on here? (*Ducks out*)

LADY ENID. (*Appearing at the door*) Oh Nicodemus. I heard a rapping, a rapping, as if someone gently tapping, tapping at my chamber door! (*She ducks out*)

NICODEMUS. (*Popping in*) There there, Lady Enid. 'Tis the wind and nothing more. (*Ducks out*)

LADY ENID. (*Popping in*) Oh Nicodemus, I was so frightened, so terribly, terribly frightened!

NICODEMUS. (*His arm comes through the door, pats her shoulder*) There there, Lady Enid. I'll never let any harm come to you.

LADY ENID. (*Kissing his hand*) Thank you, Nicodemus. Thank you.

NICODEMUS. There there. (*His hand is withdrawn and reappears as a wolf's hand. Pats her cheek and squeezes her breast*) There there.

LADY ENID. (*Reenters the room, closing the French doors behind her*) It's so good to know he's there! Is it possible my mind is affected? Or can I trust my senses five? I saw it with my very eyes. And yet, the mummy case is perfectly empty! (*Opens the mummy case.*)

JANE. (*In her maid's uniform once again, comes running out of the mummy case shrieking and wielding a meat axe.*)

LADY ENID. (*Screams and runs out the door down right, slamming it behind her. The corner of her robe sticks out through the closed door.*)

JANE. (*Flies to the door, finds it locked, and rants*) Open the door. Open the door, Lady Enid. It's just a matter of time before I get in, you know. It was the same way when I killed Lady Irma. She was all alone in the house the night I strangled her.

LADY ENID. (*Off*) No no! You're horrible!

JANE. And Victor, the little bastard. I drowned him in the mill run.

LADY ENID. (*Off*) No!

JANE. You should have seen the bubbles coming out of his ugly little nose.

LADY ENID. (*Off*)How could you? How could you?

JANE. Ah, glorious death. Glorious, glorious death!

(Nicodemus, as werewolf, bursts through French doors.)

JANE. Victor!

(Nicodemus grabs Jane by the throat, and drags her out the way he came in, howling.)

LADY ENID. (*Off*) Edgar, is that you?

(Lord Edgar rushes in and fires shots. The werewolf falls, and turns into Nicodemus.)

NICODEMUS. Each man kills the thing he loves. The coward does it with a kiss, the brave man with a sword. Yet, Nicodemus did love.

LORD EDGAR. Nicodemus, Nicodemus, I've killed you. In earnest.

NICODEMUS. Thank you. (*Dies.*)

LORD EDGAR. The poor man is dead. From his fair and unpolluted flesh may violets spring! Bury him on the moors he loved so well, and may his soul ascend to heaven, for he lived in hell!

(Blackout.)

SCENE 2

Lights up on Lady Enid and Lord Edgar. Edgar is sitting in his chair. Enid is standing beside him.

LADY ENID. Poor Nicodemus. Poor Victor. Poor Irma. Poor Jane! Somehow it just doesn't make sense.

LORD EDGAR. Enid, there are more things on heaven and earth than are dreamed of in our philosophies! Enid, I had an uncanny experience in Egypt. And I've written it all up in a treatise, which I expect will cause some stir. My very reputation as an Egyptologist would hang in the balance. I've been warned by all my colleagues not to publish it, but I must. They say that it couldn't have happened. That an ancient mummy, a hideously shriveled, decayed object, could not have survived the ages and been brought to life by spells and incantations. And yet I saw it with my very eyes! I must tell the world, even if it ruins my reputation! For I believe that we all lived before, in another time, in another age, and that you and I were lovers in ancient Egypt, thirty-five hundred years ago. She was so like you. You are so like her. Oh Enid, Enid!

LADY ENID. Stop! I can't bear it! I can't go on. Oh, you poor, poor man!

LORD EDGAR. What do you mean, Enid?

LADY ENID. Oh, stop. You're making me weep so terribly! I've done a terrible thing. I fear you'll never forgive me for it.

LORD EDGAR. What are you talking about?

LADY ENID. It was me in the tomb, Edgar.

LORD EDGAR. You? Impossible. But you were away in a sanitarium.

LADY ENID. No, I wasn't. I feigned madness. Alcazar is my father! He is actually Professor Lionel Cuncliff of Cambridge University.

LORD EDGAR. Not *the* Lionel Cuncliff! The leading Egyptologist and sarcophogologist.

LADY ENID. Yes, your old rival.

LORD EDGAR. Old Cuncliff your father? That's impossible! You couldn't have been in Egypt!

LADY ENID. If you could only believe that I did it for you, to win you away from...her. If I could make you believe that our love was destined, I thought I could bind you to me. But my father used it for his own purposes. To make a fool of you. To discredit you before the academic community and the world! He had never forgiven you for having won the Yolanda Sonabend fellowship he had so counted on. Can you ever forgive me?

LORD EDGAR. I can't believe that you pulled it off! How did you get in the tomb?

LADY ENID. The tomb was actually an Egyptian restaurant that had been closed quite a number of years. I simply came in through the kitchen.

LORD EDGAR. You little witch!

LADY ENID. We had only a few days to make it look like a tomb. We used a decorator from the theatre. Oh, the hours he spent polishing that floor. It gave us quite a turn when you discovered that footprint. But by then you wanted to believe so much, you convinced yourself. Can you ever forgive me?

LORD EDGAR. Forgive you? I want to thank you. You've freed me at last. Somehow I've come to realize that we are all God's creatures every one of us. Big Victor and little Victor too.

LADY ENID. You can say that.

LORD EDGAR. I mean it. Oh God I've been so selfish.

LADY ENID. Me too. But we can make it all up somehow.

LORD EDGAR. There's a hard day's work ahead of us Enid.

LADY ENID. But on the seventh day we'll rest.

LORD EDGAR. (*Quietly, very moved*) And in that

stillness perhaps we'll hear the spirits visiting.

LADY ENID. (*In a whisper*) Spirits?

LORD EDGAR. (*As before*) Yes, perhaps they'll be all around us—those we've lost.

LADY ENID. Big Victor and little Victor too?

LORD EDGAR. Yes, it may be that now and then throughout our lives we may still catch glimpses of them. (*Ardently*) If only I knew where to look. Where should I look, Enid?

LADY ENID. (*Going to the doors and opening them*) Out there through the fog—beyond the moors. (*Reaches out her hand to him and beckons him to come.*)

LORD EDGAR. (*His eyes fixed on her, he moves toward her slowly*) Beyond the moors?

LADY ENID. And upward . . .

LORD EDGAR. Yes, yes, upward.

LADY ENID. Toward the stars and toward that great silence.

LORD EDGAR. (*Taking her hand in his*) Thank you.

(*They stand in the doorway with their backs to us, looking up as the lights fade to darkness.*)

THE END

Costume Plot
"The Mystery of Irma Vep"
from the original production

We choose the 1890's as the period, as we needed long skirts to cover the underdressed costumes.

Shoes—One pair apiece.

I chose knee-high riding boots for Edgar, which did not show under Jane's dress, and a simple pair of black lace-up oxford-type shoes on Nicodemus and Lady Enid. They also do not show under Enid's dresses. However they should not be so bulky as to impede graceful movement of Enid.

No jewelry unless it is built onto the costumes themselves. There is absolutely no time to change anything but the costume.

Hair—The male characters should keep hair short and neatly trimmed as there is no time to adjust it under the wigs. There is barely time to think during these changes. Charles kept the hair on the sides of his head a little long so as to be pasted up into "wings" which were very effective on Nicodemus.

Wigs—For Jane I chose red hair in a bun which plays the entire show with the exception of a long loose wig when Jane appears in her nightgown in her last scenes in the first act.

For Enid I chose strawberry blond hair in a Gibson girl do which plays the entire show except when she appears in her robe and nightgown. Then she wore it hanging down loose with some loose ringlets added for glamour. I would use hair colors that were oposite the hair colors of the male characters.

I will now discuss the actual costumes themselves.

First of all, I would like to mention some things to

avoid in the construction of the costumes which I learned.

Avoid box-pleating where the sleeve meets the cuff. Though it is stylish and attractive it can cause the actor's finger to get caught in the pleats, costing precious time. So use only straight lines.

Avoid pointed bodices on the dresses as sometimes in the rush of things the dress does not go on exactly straight and a pointed bodice will betray this.

Lord Edgar: 1) I chose a Norfolk jacket which closed all the way to the neck, and matching trousers tucked into riding boots. I chose this particular jacket because there is only time to put on one garment during this change.

The boots and pants are underdressed for the entire first act. The jacket is closed with Velcro and the buttons are sewn on the overlapping panel of the jacket.

A continuous strip of Velcro will cause the jacket to bulge. I used 3-inch pieces spaced out down the length of the garment.

2) Old-fashioned undershirt for when the changes speed up in the act. It is underdressed of course. You will need two, one for each act, as they get very wet. It gets hot out there.

3) Robe

4) Lord Edgar in Egypt. Pith helmet. Safari jacket and pants. Shirt and tie.

5) Turtle neck shirt with same pants as Act I.

Be sure that the collar of turtleneck is not too wide as it will not hide under Jane's dress. Again you'll need more than one unless you wash it out every night.

Nicodemus: He has only one costume throughout the play.

I used a ratty coat with a capelet to which I attached a shirt collar and lace. It must be in one piece.

It fastens with 2 large buttons.

Velcro won't work as Nicodemus is very active and this is his only costume.

The collar *is* fastened with Velcro, however.

Robes for Enid and Jane: I gave Jane a large blanket to wrap around herself (which also covers the opening at back of gown).

I gave Enid a long robe with a train. (Also covers opening of nightgown.)

Dresses for Enid and Jane: Dresses open in the back and are fastened with Velcro from the neck to the waist.

I also added an extra width of fabric which is wrapped around the waist inside the dress and fastened with Velcro. This eliminates the split up the back and allows total freedom of movement. I'd say enough fabric to wrap to the front of the hip bone.

Vep Prop List

ACT I

Preset
Two antique guns in box.
Empty vase.
Figurine.
Book for bookcase.
Ghost candle.
Poker in stand.
Painting of Irma Vep.
Letter (*flash paper*).
Matches with striker.
Lady Enid dummy.
Wolf.
Tea tray with pot, one cup, saucer, spoon.
Red cloth.
Sewing basket with scissors, sewing and loose needles,
    bottle and cork.
Toddy saucepan.
Jane's key ring.
Jane's duster.
Loose roses.

ACT II

Preset
Scroll in mummy's hand, ring on hand.
Edgar's Egyptian costume in basket.

Shoulder bag.
Wine flask and cork.
Sher biddies (*cigarettes*).

Box of matches.
Money.
Electric torches.

ACT III

Preset
Lady Enid painting.
Wolf mask with hand-gloves.

Knife.
Irma Vep mask.
Nosferatu mask.
Blood spot.
Pentagram.
Wolfsbane.
Two dulcimers.
Meat cleaver.

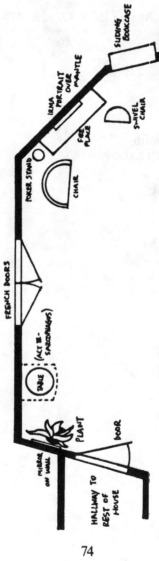

MANDACREST DROP

MIRROR ON WALL

PLANT

DOOR

HALLWAY TO REST OF HOUSE

TABLE (ACT III-SARCOPHAGUS)

FRENCH DOORS

POKER STAND

CHAIR

IRMA PORTRAIT OVER MANTLE

FIRE PLACE

SWIVEL CHAIR

SLIDING BOOKCASE

SCENE DESIGN
"THE MYSTERY OF IRMA VEP"
ACTS I & III

74

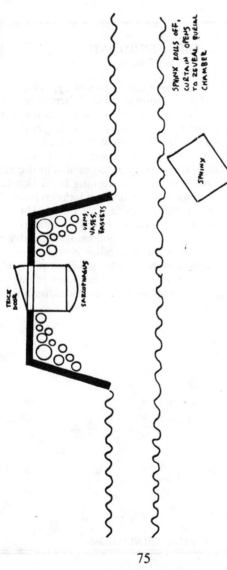

SCENE DESIGN
"THE MYSTERY OF IRMA VEP"
ACT II

TRICK DOOR

URNS, VASES, BASKETS

SARCOPHAGUS

SPHINX ROLLS OFF, CURTAIN OPENS TO REVEAL BURIAL CHAMBER

SPHINX

75

TREASURE ISLAND
Ken Ludwig

All Groups / Adventure / 10m, 1f (doubling) / Areas

Based on the masterful adventure novel by Robert Louis Stevenson, *Treasure Island* is a stunning yarn of piracy on the tropical seas. It begins at an inn on the Devon coast of England in 1775 and quickly becomes an unforgettable tale of treachery and mayhem featuring a host of legendary swashbucklers including the dangerous Billy Bones (played unforgettably in the movies by Lionel Barrymore), the sinister two-timing Israel Hands, the brassy woman pirate Anne Bonney, and the hideous form of evil incarnate, Blind Pew. At the center of it all are Jim Hawkins, a 14-year-old boy who longs for adventure, and the infamous Long John Silver, who is a complex study of good and evil, perhaps the most famous hero-villain of all time. Silver is an unscrupulous buccaneer-rogue whose greedy quest for gold, coupled with his affection for Jim, cannot help but win the heart of every soul who has ever longed for romance, treasure and adventure.

BLUE YONDER
Kate Aspengren

Dramatic Comedy / Monolgues and scenes
12f (can be performed with as few as 4 with doubling) / Unit Set

A familiar adage states, "Men may work from sun to sun, but women's work is never done." In Blue Yonder, the audience meets twelve mesmerizing and eccentric women including a flight instructor, a firefighter, a stuntwoman, a woman who donates body parts, an employment counselor, a professional softball player, a surgical nurse professional baseball player, and a daredevil who plays with dynamite among others. Through the monologues, each woman examines her life's work and explores the career that she has found. Or that has found her.

Printed in the USA
CPSIA information can be obtained
at www.ICGtesting.com
LVHW010939030124
767987LV00004B/568

9 780573 640469